To my brother Bernat

First published 2015 by Macmillan Children's Books.
This edition published 2019 by Macmillan Children's Books,
an imprint of Pan Macmillan,
20 New Wharf Road, London N1 9RR
Associated companies throughout the world
www.panmacmillan.com

ISBN: 978-1-5290-2321-3

Text and illustrations copyright © Marta Altés 2015

The right of Marta Altés to be identified as the author
and illustrator of this work has been asserted by
her in accordance with the Copyright,
Designs and Patents Act 1988.

Thanks to my editor Emily Ford and designer Sharon King-Chai

1 3 5 7 9 8 6 4 2

A CIP catalogue record for this book is available from the British Library.

Printed in China

THE KING CAT

marta altés

MACMILLAN CHILDREN'S BOOKS

I am a cat and I am the king of this house.

I do so much for my people.
I keep them entertained.

And I sleep in the day

so I can protect them at night.

All I ask for in return is some help to relax every now and again.

I am such a GOOD king.

AND

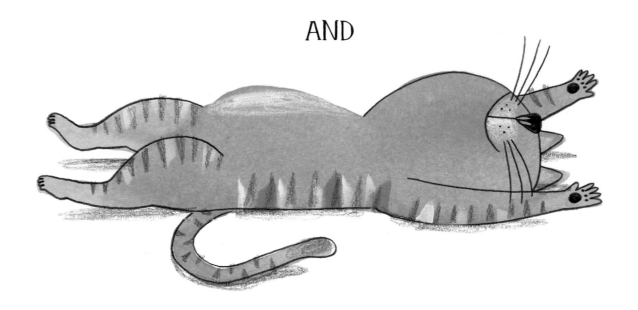

I'M

SUPER CUTE!

But something happened this morning . . .
I don't know what, but I MUST have done
something to upset my people.

If not, why OH WHY
would they have done . . .

THIS

TO ME?

Nobody even asked for my opinion.
A goldfish would have been ok, but a dog?

Dogs are annoying

dogs are strange

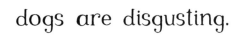

dogs are disgusting.

And let's be honest . . .

. . . dogs are quite stupid.

But as I am such a GOOD king,
I have given him a proper welcome.

But he doesn't seem to understand . . .

the rules   of MY   HOUSE.

And it looks like everyone else has forgotten too.

I don't understand.

Don't they love me any more?

Could it be true?

NO! OK, ENOUGH!
I am STILL the king of this house.

And I don't want
YOU here.

It worked!

Finally

everything

is back

to normal.

Nice and quiet . . .

But is it too quiet?

I suppose my rules are back . . .

NO!

THEY ARE NOT!

But that's ok.
We can make some new rules.

We'll make them both together.

As long as he knows I'm STILL the king.